DOVER · THRIFT · EDITIONS

Antigone

SOPHOCLES

DOVER PUBLICATIONS, INC.
New York

DOVER THRIFT EDITIONS

EDITOR: STANLEY APPELBAUM

Performance

This Dover Thrift Edition may be used in its entirety, in adaptation or in any other way for theatrical productions, professional and amateur, in the United States, without fee, permission or acknowledgment. (This may not apply outside of the United States, as copyright conditions may vary.)

Bibliographical Note

This Dover edition, first published in 1993, is an unabridged republication of the play *Antigone* from the volume *The Dramas of Sophocles Rendered in English Verse Dramatic & Lyric by Sir George Young*, as published by J. M. Dent & Sons, Ltd., London, in 1906. (The Dent edition was the second, the first having been published by George Bell & Sons, London, in 1888.) See the new Note, specially written for the Dover edition, for further details.

Library of Congress Cataloging-in-Publication Data

Sophocles.
   [Antigone. English]
   Antigone / Sophocles.
      p.   cm. — (Dover thrift editions)
   ISBN 0-486-27804-2 (pbk.)
   1. Antigone (Greek mythology)—Drama.   I. Title.   II. Series.
PA4414.A7B7   1993
882'.01—dc20
                                     93-19260
                                         CIP

Manufactured in the United States of America
Dover Publications, Inc., 31 East 2nd Street, Mineola, N.Y. 11501

Note

SOPHOCLES (born ca. 496 B.C., died after 413) was one of the three major authors of Greek tragedy. Of his 123 plays, only seven survive in full. *Antigone*, written and first performed in the late 440s B.C., is among his most often revived plays; its strong roles, and its conflict between individual morality (championed by a brave young woman) and the overbearing political needs of the state, have never lost their compelling interest through the generations.

Although the events of *Antigone* concern the family of Oedipus and follow those of *Oedipus Rex* in logical time, the latter play postdates *Antigone* by over ten years. (*Oedipus Colonus*, in turn, dates from Sophocles' extreme old age; the three plays in no way form a trilogy.)

The translation by Sir George Young (1837–1930) is not only very accurate; it also preserves the feeling of the original Greek to a great extent. The verse forms are reasonable English equivalents; the diction—lightly archaic in the blank-verse dialogues, heightened and more involuted in the stanzaic choruses—admirably reflects the hieratic nature of Sophocles' drama.

In the present edition, Sir George's own notes (exclusively concerned with problems of the Greek text and its interpretation) have been omitted. Several new, very brief footnotes have been added, identifying some Greek terms and concepts for readers less familiar with classical mythology and lore.

To avoid even more disruptive footnoting, there now follows a brief summary of the legendary events leading up to the action of the play. When Oedipus, ruler of the city-state of Thebes, learned that he had killed his father and married his mother, he blinded himself, and his wife

Jocasta killed herself. (They had had four children, the sons Eteocles and Polynices and the daughters Antigone and Ismene.) Oedipus lived on in the palace, where, vexed by the disobedience of his sons, he placed a curse on them to the effect that they would destroy each other. Indeed, they quarreled over supremacy in the city. Agreeing to govern in alternate years, they drew lots and the first year fell to Eteocles. Polynices, suspecting his brother's intentions, fled to the city of Argos, where he became son-in-law of its ruler, Adrastus. They prepared an invasion of Thebes, in association with other heroes (the Seven Against Thebes), each of the seven attacking a different gate of the city. All the invaders perished; the two brothers killed each other. Now Creon, Jocasta's brother, taking over the reins of government, has forbidden the burial of the traitor Polynices. (This was a terrible punishment, striking at the most elemental Greek feelings concerning the proper treatment of the dead; hence Antigone's irresistible urge to cover the body at least symbolically, with a handful of earth.)

Persons Represented

ANTIGONE, }
ISMENE,   } *daughters of Oedipus, late king of Thebes.*

CREON, *brother to Jocasta, late queen of Thebes, Captain-general of the army, and successor to the throne.*

A *Sentinel.*

HÆMON, *son to Creon, betrothed to Antigone.*

TIRESIAS, *a seer.*

A *Messenger in attendance on Creon.*

EURYDICE, *wife to Creon.*

The CHORUS *is composed of Senators of Thebes.*

Guards; Attendants; a Boy leading Tiresias.

Antigone

Antigone

Scene, before the Royal Palace at Thebes. Time, early morning. Enter ANTIGONE *and* ISMENE.

ANTIGONE.   Ismene, dear in very sisterhood,
   Do you perceive how Heaven upon us two
   Means to fulfil, before we come to die,
   Out of all ills that grow from Œdipus—
   What not, indeed ? for there's no sorrow or harm,
   No circumstance of scandal or of shame
   I have not seen, among your griefs, and mine.
   And now again, what is this word they say
   Our Captain-general proclaimed but now
   To the whole city ? Did you hear and heed ?
   Or are you blind, while pains of enemies
   Are passing on your friends ?

ISMENE.   Antigone,
   To me no tidings about friends are come,
   Pleasant or grievous, ever since we two
   Of our two brothers were bereft, who died
   Both in one day, each by the other's hand.
   And since the Argive host in this same night
   Took itself hence, I have heard nothing else,
   To make me happier, or more miserable.

ANTIGONE.   I knew as much; and for that reason made you
   Go out of doors—to tell you privately.

ISMENE. What is it ? I see you have some mystery.

ANTIGONE.   What ! has not Creon to the tomb preferred
                One of our brothers, and with contumely
                Withheld it from the other ?   Eteocles
                Duly, they say, even as by law was due,
                He hid beneath the earth, rendering him honour
                Among the dead below ; but the dead body
                Of Polynices, miserably slain,
                They say it has been given out publicly
                None may bewail, none bury, all must leave
                Unwept, unsepulchred, a dainty prize
                For fowl that watch, gloating upon their prey !
                This is the matter he has had proclaimed—
                Excellent Creon ! for your heed, they say,
                And mine, I tell you—mine ! and he moves hither,
                Meaning to announce it plainly in the ears
                Of such as do not know it, and to declare
                It is no matter of small moment ; he
                Who does any of these things shall surely die ;
                The citizens shall stone him in the streets.
                So stands the case.   Now you will quickly show
                If you are worthy of your birth or no.
ISMENE.   But O rash heart, what good, if it be thus,
                Could I effect, helping or hindering ?
ANTIGONE.   Look, will you join me ? will you work with me ?
ISMENE. In what attempt ? What mean you ?
ANTIGONE.   Help me lift
                The body up—
ISMENE.   What, would you bury him ?
                Against the proclamation ?
ANTIGONE.   My own brother
                And yours I will ! If you will not, I will ;
                I shall not prove disloyal.
ISMENE.   You are mad !
                When Creon has forbidden it ?

ANTIGONE. From mine own
He has no right to stay me.
ISMENE. Alas, O sister,
Think how our father perished ! self-convict—
Abhorred—dishonoured—blind—his eyes put out
By his own hand ! How she who was at once
His wife and mother with a knotted noose
Laid violent hands on her own life ! And how
Our two unhappy brothers in one day
Each on his own head by the other's hand
Wrought common ruin ! We now left alone—
Do but consider how most miserably
We too shall perish, if despite of law
We traverse the behest or power of kings.
We must remember we are women born,
Unapt to cope with men ; and, being ruled
By mightier than ourselves, we have to hear
These things—and worse. For my part, I will ask
Pardon of those beneath, for what perforce
I needs must do, but yield obedience
To them that walk in power ; to exceed
Is madness, and not wisdom.
ANTIGONE. Then in future
I will not bid you help me ; nor henceforth,
Though you desire, shall you, with my good will,
Share what I do. Be what seems right to you ;
Him will I bury. Death, so met, were honour ;
And for that capital crime of piety,
Loving and loved, I will lie by his side.
Far longer is there need I satisfy
Those nether Powers, than powers on earth ; for there
For ever must I lie. You, if you will,
Hold up to scorn what is approved of Heaven !
ISMENE. I am not one to cover things with scorn ;

But I was born too feeble to contend
Against the state.

ANTIGONE.   Yes, you can put that forward ;
But I will go and heap a burial mound
Over my most dear brother.

ISMENE.   My poor sister,
How beyond measure do I fear for you !

ANTIGONE.   Do not spend fear on me. Shape your own course.

ISMENE. At least announce it, then, to nobody,
But keep it close, as I will.

ANTIGONE.   Tell it, tell it !
You'll cross me worse, by far, if you keep silence—
Not publish it to all.

ISMENE.   Your heart beats hotly
For chilling work !

ANTIGONE.   I know that those approve
Whom I most need to please.

ISMENE.   If you could do it !
But you desire impossibilities.

ANTIGONE.   Well, when I find I have no power to stir,
I will cease trying.

ISMENE.   But things impossible
'Tis wrong to attempt at all.

ANTIGONE.   If you will say it,
I shall detest you soon ;   and you will justly
Incur the dead man's hatred.   Suffer me
And my unwisdom to endure the weight
Of what is threatened.   I shall meet with nothing
More grievous, at the worst, than death, with honour.

ISMENE. Then go, if you will have it :   and take this with you,
You go on a fool's errand !   [*Exit* ANTIGONE.
                                    Lover true
To your beloved, none the less, are you !   [*Exit.*

Enter THEBAN SENATORS, *as Chorus.*

CHORUS.

I. 1.

Sunbeam bright !   Thou fairest ray
    That ever dawned on Theban eyes
        Over the portals seven !
O orb of aureate day,
    How glorious didst thou rise
        O'er Dirca's[1] streams, shining from heaven,
Him, the man[2] with shield of white
Who came from Argos in armour dight
Hurrying runagate o'er the plain,[3]
Jerking harder his bridle rein ;
Who by Polynices' quarrellous broil
Stirred up in arms to invade our soil
        With strident cries as an eagle flies
        Swooped down on the fields before him,
'Neath cover of eagle pinion white
As drifted snow, a buckler bright
        On many a breast, and a horsetail crest
        From each helm floating o'er him.

I. 2.

Yawning with many a blood-stained spear
    Around our seven-gated town
        High o'er the roofs he stood ;
Then, or ever a torch could sear

[1] Spring and river at Thebes.
[2] Adrastus, one of the seven leaders of the invaders of Thebes.
[3] The orb is hurrying the man into retreat.

With flames the rampart-crown—
    Or ever his jaws were filled with blood
Of us and ours, lo, he was fled !
Such clatter of war behind him spread,
Stress too sore for his utmost might
Matched with the Dragon[1] in the fight ;
For Zeus abhors tongue-glorious boasts ;
And straightway as he beheld their hosts,
Where on they rolled, covered with gold,
    Streaming in mighty eddy,
Scornfully with a missile flame
He struck down Capaneus,[2] as he came
Uplifting high his victory-cry
    At the topmost goal already.

II. 1.

Tantalus-like[3] aloft he hung, then fell ;
    Earth at his fall resounded ;
Even as, maddened by the Bacchic spell,
    On with torch in hand he bounded,
      Breathing blasts of hate.
So the stroke was turned aside,
    Mighty Ares rudely dealing
Others elsewhere, far and wide,
    Like a right-hand courser wheeling
      Round the goals of fate.

For captains seven at portals seven
Found each his match in the combat even,
And left on the field both sword and shield

[1] The Thebans, descendants of men generated from dragon's teeth.
[2] Another of the Seven Against Thebes.
[3] Like Tantalus, tormented by hunger and thirst in the underworld.

As a trophy to Zeus, who o'erthrew them ;
Save the wretched twain, who against each other
Though born of one father, and one mother,
Laid lances at aim—to their own death came,
    And the common fate that slew them.

II. 2.

But now loud Victory returns at last
        On Theban chariots smiling,
Let us begin oblivion of the past,
        Memories of the late war beguiling
            Into slumber sound.
        Seek we every holy shrine ;
            There begin the night-long chorus ;
        Let the Theban Boy divine,
            Bacchus, lead the way before us,
                Shaking all the ground.

Leave we the song : the King is here ;
Creon, Menœceus' son, draws near ;
To the function strange—like the heaven-sent change
    Which has raised him newly to power :
What counsel urging—what ends of state,
That he summons us to deliberate,
The elders all, by his herald's call,
    At a strange unwonted hour ?

Enter CREON, *attended.*

CREON.   Sirs, for the ship of state—the Gods once more,
        After much rocking on a stormy surge,
        Set her on even keel.   Now therefore you,
        You of all others, by my summoners
        I bade come hither ;   having found you first
        Right loyal ever to the kingly power

In Laius' time ;   and next, while Œdipus
Ordered the commonwealth ;   and since his fall,
With steadfast purposes abiding still,
Circling their progeny.   Now, since they perished,
Both on one day, slain by a two-edged fate,
Striking and stricken, sullied with a stain
Of mutual fratricide, I, as you know,
In right of kinship nearest to the dead,
Possess the throne and take the supreme power.
Howbeit it is impossible to know
The spirit of any man, purpose or will,
Before it be displayed by exercise
In government and laws.   To me, I say,
Now as of old, that pilot of the state
Who sets no hand to the best policy,
But remains tongue-tied through some terror, seems
Vilest of men.   Him too, who sets a friend
Before his native land, I prize at nothing.
God, who seest all things always, witness it !
If I perceive, where safety should have been,
Mischief advancing toward my citizens,
I will not sit in silence ;   nor account
As friend to me the country's enemy ;
But thus I deem :   she is our ark of safety ;
And friends are made then only, when, embarked
Upon her deck, we ride the seas upright.
Such are the laws by which I mean to further
This city's welfare ;   and akin to these
I have given orders to the citizens
Touching the sons of Œdipus.   Eteocles,
Who in this city's quarrel fought and fell,
The foremost of our champions in the fray,
They should entomb with the full sanctity
Of rites that solemnize the downward road

Of their dead greatest.   Him the while, his brother,
That Polynices who, returning home
A banished man, sought to lay waste with fire
His household Gods, his native country—sought
To glut himself with his own kindred's blood,
Or carry them away to slavery,
It has been promulgated to the city
No man shall bury, none should wail for him ;
Unsepulchred, shamed in the eyes of men,
His body shall be left to be devoured
By dogs and fowls of the air.   Such is my will.
Never with me shall wicked men usurp
The honours of the righteous ;   but whoe'er
Is friendly to this city shall, by me,
Living or dead, be honoured equally.

1 SENATOR.   Creon Menœceus' son, we hear your pleasure
Both on this city's friend, and on her foe ;
It is your sovereignty's prerogative
To pass with absolute freedom on the dead,
And us, who have survived them.

CREON.   Please to see
What has been said performed.

1 SENATOR.   That charge confer
On some one who is younger.

CREON.   Of the body ?
Sentries are set, already.

1 SENATOR.   Then what else
Is there, besides, which you would lay on us ?

CREON.   Not to connive at disobedience.

1 SENATOR.   There's no such fool as to embrace his death.

CREON.   Death is the penalty.   But men right often
Are brought to ruin, through their dreams of gain.

Enter a Sentinel.

SENTINEL. My lord, I will not say—" breathless with speed
            I come, plying a nimble foot ; "   for truly
            I had a many sticking-points of thought,
            Wheeling about to march upon my rear.
            For my heart whispered me all sorts of counsel ;
            " Poor wretch, why go, to meet thy sentence ? "—
                " Wretch,
            Tarrying again ?   If Creon hear the news
            From others' lips, how shalt thou then not rue it ? "
            Out of this whirligig it came to pass
            I hastened—at my leisure ; a short road,
            Thus, becomes long.   Nevertheless at last
            It won the day to come hither, to your presence ;
            And speak I will, though nothing have to say ;
            For I come clinging to the hope that I
            Can suffer nothing—save my destiny.
CREON.   Well—and what caused you this disheartenment ?
SENTINEL.   First let me tell you what concerns myself.
            I do protest, I neither did the deed,
            Nor saw it done, whoever 'twas who did it ;
            Nor should I rightly come to any harm.
CREON.   At all events you are a good tactician,
            And fence the matter off all round.   But clearly
            You have some strange thing to tell ?
SENTINEL.   Yes.   Serious tidings
            Induce much hesitation.
CREON.   Once for all
            Please to speak out, and make an end, and go.
SENTINEL.   Why, I am telling you.   That body some one
            Has just now buried—sprinkled thirsty dust
            Over the form—added the proper rites,
            And has gone off.
CREON.   What say you ?   What man dared
            To do it ?

SENTINEL.   I know not.   There was no dint there
           Of any mattock, not a sod was turned ;
           Merely hard ground and bare, without a break,
           Without a rut from wheels ;   it was some workman
           Who left no mark.   When the first day-sentry
           Shewed what had happened, we were all dismayed.
           The body had vanished ;   not indeed interred,
           But a light dust lay on it, as if poured out
           By one who shunned the curse ;   and there appeared
           No trace that a wild beast, or any hound,
           Had come, or torn the carcase.   Angry words
           Were bandied up and down, guard blaming guard,
           And blows had like to end it, none being by
           To hinder ;   for each one of us in turn
           Stood culprit, none convicted, but the plea
           " I know not " passed.   Ready were we to take
           Hot iron in hand, or pass through fire, and call
           The Gods to witness, that we neither did it,
           Nor were accessory to any man
           Who compassed it, or did it.   So at last,
           When all our searching proved to be in vain,
           There speaks up one, who made us, every man,
           Hang down our heads for fear, knowing no way
           To say him nay, or without scathe comply.
           His burden was, this business must be carried
           To you, without reserve.   That voice prevailed ;
           And me, poor wretch, the lot condemns to get
           This piece of luck.   I come a post unwilling,
           I well believe it, to unwilling ears ;
           None love the messenger who brings bad news.
1 SENATOR.   My lord, my heart misgave me from the first
           This must be something more than natural.
CREON.   Truce to your speech, before I choke with rage,
           Lest you be found at once grey-beard and fool !

To say that guardian deities would care
For this dead body, is intolerable.
Could they, by way of supereminent honour
Paid to a benefactor, give him burial,
Who came to fire their land, their pillared fanes
And sacred treasures, and set laws at nought ?
Or do you see Gods honouring the bad ?
'Tis false.   These orders from the first some people
Hardly accepted, murmuring at me,
Shaking their heads in secret, stiffening
Uneasy necks against this yoke of mine.
They have suborned these sentinels to do it,
I know that well.   No such ill currency
Ever appeared, as money to mankind :
This is it that sacks cities, this routs out
Men from their homes, and trains and turns astray
The minds of honest mortals, setting them
Upon base actions ;   this made plain to men
Habits of all misdoing, and cognizance
Of every work of wickedness.   Howbeit
Such hireling perpetrators, in the end,
Have wrought so far, that they shall pay for it.
So surely as I live to worship Jove,
Know this for truth ;   I swear it in your ears ;
Except you find and bring before my face
The real actor in this funeral,
Death, by itself, shall not suffice for you,
Before, hung up alive, you have revealed
The secret of this outrage ;   that henceforth
You may seek plunder—not without respect
Of where your profit lies ;   and may be taught
It is not good to covet all men's pay ;
For mark you !   by corruption few men thrive,
And many come to mischief.

SENTINEL.   Have I leave
          To say a word, or shall I turn and go ?
CREON.   Cannot you see your prating tortures me ?
SENTINEL.   Pricks you how deep ?   In the ears, or to the spleen ?
CREON.   Why do you gauge my chafing, where it lies ?
SENTINEL.   Your heart-ache were the doer's, your ear-ache mine.
CREON.   Out, what a bare-faced babbler born art thou!
SENTINEL.   Never the actor in this business, though!
CREON.   Yes, and for money you would sell your soul!
SENTINEL.   Plague on it! 'tis hard, a man should be suspicious,
          And with a false suspicion !
CREON.   Yes, suspicion ;
          Mince it as best you may. Make me to know
          Whose are these doings, or you shall soon allow
          Left-handed gains work their own punishment.   [*Exit.*
SENTINEL.   I wish he may be found. Chance must decide,
          Whether or no, you will not, certainly,
          See me returning hither. Heaven be praised
          I am in safety, past all thought or dream!   [*Exit.*

CHORUS

I. 1.

          Much is there passing strange ;
              Nothing surpassing mankind.
          He it is loves to range
          Over the ocean hoar,
          Thorough the surges' roar,
              South winds raging behind ;

          Earth, too, wears he away,
              The Mother of Gods on high,
          Tireless, free from decay ;
          With team he furrows the ground,

And the ploughs go round and round,
  As year on year goes by.

I. 2.

The bird-tribes, light of mind,
  The races of beasts of prey,
And sea-fish after their kind,
Man, abounding in wiles,
Entangles in his toils
  And carries captive away.

The roamers over the hill,
  The field-inhabiting deer,
By craft he conquers, at will ;
He bends beneath his yoke
The neck of the steed unbroke,
  And pride of the upland steer.

II. 1.

He has gotten him speech, and fancy breeze-betost,
  And for the state instinct of order meet ;
He has found him shelter from the chilling frost
  Of a clear sky, and from the arrowy sleet ;
Illimitable in cunning, cunning-less
  He meets no change of fortune that can come ;
He has found escape from pain and helplessness ;
  Only he knows no refuge from the tomb.

II. 2.

Now bends he to the good, now to the ill,
  With craft of art, subtle past reach of sight ;

Wresting his country's laws to his own will,
  Spurning the sanctions of celestial right ;
High in the city, he is made city-less,
  Whoso is corrupt, for his impiety ;
He that will work the works of wickedness,
  Let him not house, let him not hold, with me !

At this monstrous vision I stand in
Doubt! How dare I say, well knowing her,
That this maid is not—Antigone !
      Daughter of Œdipus !
Hapless child, of a hapless father !
Sure—ah surely they did not find thee
Madly defying our king's commandments,
  And so prisoner bring thee here ?

Enter Sentinel with ANTIGONE.

SENTINEL.   This is the woman who has done the deed.
      We took her burying him. Where's Creon ?
1 SENATOR.   Here
      Comes he again, out of the house, at need.

Enter CREON.

CREON. What is it ? In what fit season come I forth ?
SENTINEL.   My lord, I see a man should never vow
      He will not do a thing, for second thoughts
      Bely the purpose. Truly I could have sworn
      It would be long indeed ere I came hither
      Under that hail of threats you rained on me.
      But since an unforeseen happy surprise
      Passes all other pleasing out of measure,
      I come, though I forswore it mightily,
      Bringing this maiden, who was caught in act
      To set that bier in order. Here, my lord,

No lot was cast ; this windfall is to me,
And to no other. Take her, now, yourself ;
Examine and convict her, as you please ;
I wash my hands of it, and ought, of right,
To be clean quit of the scrape, for good and all.

CREON. You seized—and bring—her ! In what way, and whence ?

SENTINEL. Burying that man, herself ! You know the whole.

CREON. Are you in earnest ? Do you understand
What you are saying ?

SENTINEL.   Yes, that I saw this girl
Burying that body you forbade to bury.
Do I speak clear and plain ?

CREON.   How might this be,
That she was seen, and taken in the act ?

SENTINEL. Why thus it happened. When we reached the place,
Wrought on by those dread menacings from you,
We swept away all dust that covered up
The body, and laid the clammy limbs quite bare,
And windward from the summit of the hill,
Out of the tainted air that spread from him,
We sat us down, each, as it might be, rousing
His neighbour with a clamour of abuse,
Wakening him up, whenever any one
Seemed to be slack in watching. This went on,
Till in mid air the luminous orb of day
Stood, and the heat grew sultry. Suddenly
A violent eddy lifted from the ground
A hurricane, a trouble of the sky ;
Ruffling all foliage of the woodland plain
It filled the horizon ; the vast atmosphere
Thickened to meet it ; we, closing our eyes,
Endured the Heaven-sent plague. After a while,
When it had ceased, there stands this maiden in sight,
And wails aloud, shrill as the bitter note

Of the sad bird, when as she finds the couch
Of her void nest robbed of her young ;   so she,
Soon as she sees the body stripped and bare,
Bursts out in shrieks, and calls down curses dire
On their heads who had done it. Straightway then
She gathers handfuls of dry dust, and brings them,
And from a shapely brazen cruse held high
She crowns the body with drink-offerings,
Once, twice, and thrice. We at the sight rushed forward,
And trapped her, nothing daunted, on the spot ;
And taxed her with the past offence, and this
The present. Not one whit did she deny ;
A pleasant though a pitiful sight to me ;
For nothing's sweeter than to have got off
In person ;   but to bring into mischance
Our friends is pitiful. And yet to pay
No more than this is cheap, to save one's life.

CREON.   Do you, I say—you, with your downcast brow—
Own or deny that you have done this deed ?

ANTIGONE.   I say I did it ;   I deny it not.

CREON.   Take yourself hence, whither you will, sir knave;
You are acquitted of a heavy charge.   [*Exit Sentinel.*
Now tell me, not at length, but in brief space,
Knew you the order not to do it ?

ANTIGONE.   Yes,
I knew it ;   what should hinder ?   It was plain.

CREON.   And you made free to overstep my law ?

ANTIGONE.   Because it was not Zeus who ordered it,
Nor Justice, dweller with the Nether Gods,
Gave such a law to men ;   nor did I deem
Your ordinance of so much binding force,
As that a mortal man could overbear
The unchangeable unwritten code of Heaven ;
This is not of today and yesterday,

But lives for ever, having origin
Whence no man knows : whose sanctions I were loath
In Heaven's sight to provoke, fearing the will
Of any man. I knew that I should die—
How otherwise ? even although your voice
Had never so prescribed. And that I die
Before my hour is due, that I count gain.
For one who lives in many ills, as I—
How should he fail to gain by dying ? Thus
To me the pain is light, to meet this fate ;
But had I borne to leave the body of him
My mother bare unburied, then, indeed,
I might feel pain ; but as it is, I cannot ;
And if my present action seems to you
Foolish—'tis like I am found guilty of folly
At a fool's mouth !

1 SENATOR.   Lo you, the spirit stout
Of her stout father's child—unapt to bend
Beneath misfortune !

CREON.   But be well assured,
Tempers too stubborn are the first to fail ;
The hardest iron from the furnace, forged
To stiffness, you may see most frequently
Shivered and broken ; and the chafing steeds
I have known governed with a slender curb.
It is unseemly that a household drudge
Should be misproud ; but she was conversant
With outrage, ever since she passed the bounds
Laid down by law ; then hard upon that deed
Comes this, the second outrage, to exult
And triumph in her deed. Truly if here
She wield such powers uncensured, she is man,
I woman! Be she of my sister born,
Or nearer to myself than the whole band

Of our domestic tutelary Jove,
She, and the sister—for her equally
I charge with compassing this funeral—
Shall not escape a most tremendous doom.
And call her ; for within the house but now
I saw her, frenzied and beside herself ;
And it is common for the moody sprite
Of plotters in the dark to no good end
To have been caught, planning its knavery,
Before the deed is acted. None the less
I hate it, when one taken in misdoing
Straight seeks to gloss the facts !

ANTIGONE.   Would you aught more
Than take my life, whom you did catch ?

CREON.   Not I ;
Take that, take all.

ANTIGONE.   Then why do you delay ?
Since naught is pleasing of your words to me,
Or, as I trust, can ever please, so mine
Must needs be unacceptable to you.
And yet from whence could I have gathered praise
More worthily, than from depositing
My own brother in a tomb ? These, all of them,
Would utter one approval, did not fear
Seal up their lips. 'Tis tyranny's privilege,
And not the least—power to declare and do
What it is minded.

CREON.   You, of all this people,
Are singular in your discernment.

ANTIGONE.   Nay,
They too discern ; they but refrain their tongues
At your behest.

CREON.   And you are not ashamed
That you deem otherwise ?

ANTIGONE. It is no shame
    To pay respect to our own flesh and blood.
CREON. And his dead foeman, was not he your brother
    As well ?
ANTIGONE. Yes, the same sire's and mother's son.
CREON. Why pay, then, honours which are wrongs to him ?
ANTIGONE. The dead clay makes no protest.
CREON. Not although
    His with a villain's share your reverence ?
ANTIGONE. It was no bondman perished, but a brother.
CREON. Spoiling, I say, this country ; while his rival
    Stood for it.
ANTIGONE. All the same, these rites are due
    To the underworld.
CREON. But not in equal measure
    Both for the good man and the bad.
ANTIGONE. Who knows
    This is not piety there ?
CREON. The enemy
    Can never be a friend, even in death.
ANTIGONE. Well, I was made for fellowship in love,
    Not fellowship in hate.
CREON. Then get you down
    Thither, and love, if you must love, the dead!
    No woman, while I live, shall order me.

CHORUS.

See where out by the doors Ismene
Weeping drops of sisterly grieving
Comes ; and a cloud o'erhanging her eyebrows
Mars her dark-flushed cheek, and moistens
    Her fair face with pitiful tears.

Enter Attendants with ISMENE.

CREON.   And you—who like a viper unawares
         Have crept into my house, and sucked me bloodless,
         While I unknowingly was fostering you,
         Twin furies, to the upsetting of my throne—
         Come, tell me, will you say you also shared
         This burying, or protest your innocence ?
ISMENE.   Yes, I have done it—if Antigone
         Says so—I join with her to share the blame.
ANTIGONE.   That justice will not suffer ;   you refused,
         And I—I had no partner.
ISMENE.   In your trouble
         I do not blush to claim companionship
         Of what you have to endure.
ANTIGONE.   Whose was the deed
         Death and the spirits of the dead can tell !
         A friend in words is not a friend for me.
ISMENE.   Shame me not, sister, by denying me
         A death, for honouring the dead, with you !
ANTIGONE.   Mix not your death with mine. Do not claim work
         You did not touch. I shall suffice to die.
ISMENE.   And what care I for life, if I lost you ?
ANTIGONE.   Ask Creon ;   you are dutiful to him.
ISMENE.   Why do you cross me so, to no good purpose ?
ANTIGONE.   Nay, I am sick at heart, if I do make
         My mock of you.
ISMENE.   Nay but what can I do,
         Now, even yet, to help you ?
ANTIGONE.   Save yourself ;
         I do not grudge you your escape.
ISMENE.   O me
         Unhappy! And must I miss to share your fate ?
ANTIGONE.   You made your choice, to live ;   I mine, to die.
ISMENE.   Not if you count my words unsaid.
ANTIGONE.   By some

Your judgment is approved ;   by others mine.
ISMENE. Then our delinquency is equal, too.
ANTIGONE.   Take courage, you are living ;   but my life
Long since has died, so I might serve the dead.
CREON. Of these two girls I swear the one even now
Has been proved witless ;   the other was so born.
ISMENE. Ah sir, the wretched cannot keep the wit
That they were born with, but it flits away.
CREON. Yours did so, when you chose to join ill-doers
In their misdoing.
ISMENE.   How could I live on
Alone, without my sister ?
CREON.   Do not say
"My sister";   for you have no sister more.
ISMENE. What, will you put to death your own son's bride ?
CREON. He may go further afield—
ISMENE.   Not as by troth
Plighted to her by him.
CREON.   Unworthy wives
For sons of mine I hate.
ANTIGONE.   O dearest Hæmon,
How are you slighted by your father !
CREON.   I
Am weary of your marriage, and of you.
ISMENE. Your own son! will you tear her from his arms ?
CREON. Death will prevent that bridal-rite, for me.
1 SENATOR.   I see, the sentence of this maiden's death
Has been determined.
CREON.   Then we see the same.
An end of trifling. Slaves, there, take them in !
As women, henceforth, must they live—not suffered
To gad abroad ;   for even bold men flinch,
When they view Death hard by the verge of Life.
                              [*Exeunt* ANTIGONE *and* ISMENE, *guarded.*

CHORUS.

I. 1.

Happy the man whose cup of life is free
　　From taste of evil ! If Heaven's influence shake them,
　No ill but follows, till it overtake them,
All generations of his family ;
　　　Like as when before the sweep
　　　　Of the sea-borne Thracian blast
　　　　The surge of ocean coursing past
　　Above the cavern of the deep
　　Rolls up from the region under
　　　All the blackness of the shore,
　　And the beaten beaches thunder
　　　Answer to the roar.

I. 2.

　　Woes upon woes on Labdacus' race[1] I see—
　　　Living or dead—inveterately descend ;
　　　And son with sire entangled, without end,
　And by some God smitten without remedy ;
　　　　For a light of late had spread
　　　　　O'er the last surviving root
　　　　In the house of Œdipus ;
　　　　Now, the sickle murderous
　　　　Of the Rulers of the dead,
　　　　And wild words beyond control,
　　　　And the frenzy of her own soul,
　　　　　Again mow down the shoot.

---

[1] Labdacus was a descendant of the founder of Thebes, and an ancestor of Oedipus.

II. 1.

Thy power, O God, what pride of man constraineth,
Which neither sleep, that all things else enchaineth,
    Nor even the tireless moons of Heaven destroy ?
        Thy throne is founded fast,
    High on Olympus, in great brilliancy,
            Far beyond Time's annoy.
    Through present and through future and through
        past
        Abideth one decree ;
            Nought in excess
Enters the life of man without unhappiness.

II. 2.

For wandering Hope to many among mankind
Seems pleasurable ;   but to many a mind
    Proves but a mockery of its wild desires.
        They know not aught, nor fear,
    Till their feet feel the pathway strewn with fires.
        "If evil good appear,
    That soul to his ruin is divinely led"—
        (Wisely the word was said !)
            And short the hour
He spends unscathed by the avenging power.

            Hæmon comes, thy last surviving
            Child. Is he here to bewail, indignant,
            His lost bride, Antigone ?   Grieves he
                For a vain promise—her marriage-bed ?

Enter HÆMON.

CREON.   We shall know soon, better than seers can tell us.
         Son, you are here in anger, are you not,
         Against your sire, hearing his final doom
         Upon your bride to be ?   Or are we friends,
         Always, with you, whate'er our policy ?
HÆMON.   Yours am I, father ;   and you guide my steps
         With your good counsels, which for my part I
         Will follow closely ;   for there is no marriage
         Shall occupy a larger place with me
         Than your direction, in the path of honour.
CREON.   So is it right, my son, to be disposed—
         In everything to back your father's quarrel.
         It is for this men pray to breed and rear
         In their homes dutiful offspring—to requite
         The foe with evil, and their father's friend
         Honour, as did their father. Whoso gets
         Children unserviceable—what else could he
         Be said to breed, but troubles for himself,
         And store of laughter for his enemies ?
         Nay, never fling away your wits, my son,
         Through liking for a woman ;   recollect,
         Cold are embracings, where the wife is naught,
         Who shares your board and bed. And what worse sore
         Can plague us, than a loved one's worthlessness ?
         Better to spurn this maiden as a foe !
         Leave her to wed some bridegroom in the grave !
         For, having caught her in the act, alone
         Of the whole city disobeying me,
         I will not publicly bely myself,
         But kill her. Now let her go glorify
         Her God of kindred !   If I choose to cherish
         My own born kinsfolk in rebelliousness,
         Then verily I must count on strangers too.
         For he alone who is a man of worth

In his own household will appear upright
In the state also ;   and whoe'er offends
Against the laws by violence, or thinks
To give commands to rulers—I deny
Favour to such. Obedience is due
To the state's officer in small and great,
Just and unjust commandments ;   he who pays it
I should be confident would govern well,
And cheerfully be governed, and abide
A true and trusty comrade at my back,
Firm in the ranks amid the storm of war.
There lives no greater fiend than Anarchy ;
She ruins states, turns houses out of doors,
Breaks up in rout the embattled soldiery ;
While Discipline preserves the multitude
Of the ordered host alive. Therefore it is
We must assist the cause of order ;   this
Forbids concession to a feminine will ;
Better be outcast, if we must, of men,
Than have it said a woman worsted us.

1 SENATOR.   Unless old age have robbed me of myself,
I think the tenor of your words is wise.

HÆMON.   Father, the Gods plant reason in mankind,
Of all good gifts the highest ;   and to say
You speak not rightly in this, I lack the power ;
Nor do I crave it. Still, another's thought
Might be of service ;   and it is for me,
Being your son, to mark the words, the deeds,
And the complaints, of all. To a private man
Your frown is dreadful, who has things to say
That will offend you ;   but I secretly
Can gather this ;   how the folk mourn this maid,
" Who of all women most unmeriting,
For noblest acts dies by the worst of deaths,

Who her own brother battle-slain—unburied—
Would not allow to perish in the fangs
Of carrion hounds or any bird of prey ;
And " (so the whisper darkling passes round)
" Is she not worthy to be carved in gold ? "
Father, beside your welfare there is nothing
More prized by me ;   for what more glorious crown
Can be to children, than their father's honour ?
Or to a father, from his sons, than theirs ?
Do not persist, then, to retain at heart
One sole idea, that the thing is right
Which your mouth utters, and nought else beside.
For all men who believe themselves alone
Wise, or that they possess a soul or speech
Such as none other, turn them inside out,
They are found empty ;   and though a man be wise,
It is no shame for him to live and learn,
And not to stretch a course too far. You see
How all the trees on winter torrent banks,
Yielding, preserve their sprays ;   those that would stem it
Break, roots and all ;   the shipman too, who keeps
The vessel's main-sheet taut, and will not slacken,
Goes cruising, in the end, keel uppermost :
Let thy wrath go !   Be willing to relent !
For if some sense, even from a younger head,
Be mine to afford, I say it is far better
A man should be, for every accident,
Furnished with inbred skill ;   but what of that ?
Since nature's bent will have it otherwise,
'Tis good to learn of those who counsel wisely.

1 SENATOR.   Sir, you might learn, when he speaks seasonably ;
And you, from him ;   for both have spoken well.

CREON.   Men that we are, must we be sent to school
To learn discretion of a boy like this ?

HÆMON.   None that's dishonest ;   and if I am young,
          It is not well to have regard to years
          Rather than services.
CREON.   Good service is it,
          To pay respect to rebels ?
HÆMON.   To wrongdoers
          I would not even ask for reverence.
CREON.   Was it not some such taint infected her ?
HÆMON.   So say not all this populace of Thebes.
CREON.   The city to prescribe me my decrees !
HÆMON.   Look, say you so, you are too young in this !
CREON.   Am I to rule this land after some will
          Other than mine ?
HÆMON.   A city is no city
          That is of one man only.
CREON.   Is not the city
          Held to be his who rules it ?
HÆMON.   That were brave—
          You, a sole monarch of an empty land !
CREON.   This fellow, it seems, fights on the woman's side.
HÆMON.   An you be woman !   My forethought is for you.
CREON.   O villain—traversing thy father's rights !
HÆMON.   Because I see you sinning against right.
CREON.   Sin I, to cause my sway to be held sacred ?
HÆMON.   You desecrate, by trampling on Heaven's honour.
CREON.   Foul spotted heart—a woman's follower !
HÆMON.   You will not find me serving what is vile.
CREON.   I say this talk of thine is all for her.
HÆMON.   And you, and me, and for the Gods beneath !
CREON.   Never shall she live on to marry thee !
HÆMON.   Die as she may, she shall not die alone.
CREON.   Art thou grown bold enough to threaten, too ?
HÆMON.   Where is the threat, to speak against vain counsel ?
CREON.   Vain boy, thyself shalt rue thy counselling.
HÆMON.   I had called you erring, were you not my sire.

CREON.   Thou woman's bondman, do not spaniel me !
HÆMON.   Do you expect to speak, and not be answered ?
CREON.   Do I so ? By Olympus over us,
            If thou revile me, and find fault with me,
            Never believe but it shall cost thee dear !
            Bring out the wretch, that in his sight, at once,
            Here, with her bridegroom by her, she may die !
HÆMON.   Not in my sight, at least—not by my side,
            Believe it, shall she perish ! And for thee—
            Storm at the friends who choose they company !
            My face thou never shalt behold again.   [Exit.
1 SENATOR.   The man is gone, my lord, headlong with rage ;
            And wits so young, when galled, are full of danger.
CREON.   Let be, let him imagine more, or do,
            Than mortal may ;   yet he shall not redeem
            From sentence those two maidens.
1 SENATOR.   Both of them ?
            Is it your will to slay them both alike ?
CREON.   That is well said ;   not her who did not touch it.
1 SENATOR.   And by what death mean you to kill the other ?
CREON.   Into some waste untrodden of mankind
            She shall be drawn, and, in some rock-hewn cave,
            With only food enough provided her
            For expiation, so that all the city
            Escape the guilt of blood, buried alive.
            There, if she ask him, Hades, the one God
            Whom she regards, may grant her not to perish ;
            Or there, at latest, she shall recognize
            It is lost labour to revere the dead.   [Exit.

CHORUS.

O Love, thou art victor in fight : thou mak'st all things afraid ;
Thou couchest thee softly at night on the cheeks of a maid ;
Thou passest the bounds of the sea, and the folds of the fields ;

To thee the immortal, to thee the ephemeral yields ;
Thou maddenest them that possess thee ;   thou turnest astray
The souls of the just, to oppress them, out of the way ;
Thou hast kindled amongst us pride, and the quarrel of kin ;
Thou art lord, by the eyes of a bride, and the love-light therein ;
Thou sittest assessor with Right ;   her kingdom is thine,
Who sports with invincible might, Aphrodita divine.

Enter ANTIGONE, *guarded*.

> I too, myself, am carried as I look
> Beyond the bounds of right ;
> Nor can I brook
> The springing fountain of my tears, to see
> My child, Antigone,
> Pass to the chamber of universal night.

I. 1.

ANTIGONE.   Behold me, people of my native land :
> I wend my latest way :
> I gaze upon the latest light of day
> That I shall ever see ;
> Death, who lays all to rest, is leading me
> To Acheron's[1] far strand
> Alive ;   to me no bridal hymns belong,
> For me no marriage song
> Has yet been sung ;   but Acheron instead
> Is it, whom I must wed.

CHORUS.   Nay but with praise and voicings of renown
> Thou partest for that prison-house of the dead ;
> Unsmitten by diseases that consume,
> By sword unvisited,

[1] River in the underworld.

Thou only of mortals freely shalt go down,
Alive, to the tomb.

I. 2.

ANTIGONE.   I have heard tell the sorrowful end of her,[1]
That Phrygian sojourner
On Sipylus' peak, offspring of Tantalus ;
How stony shoots upgrown
Like ivy bands enclosed her in the stone ;
With snows continuous
And ceaseless rain her body melts away ;
Streams from her tear-flown head
Water her front ;   likest to hers the bed
My fate prepares today.

CHORUS.   She was of godlike nature, goddess-sprung,
And we are mortals, and of human race ;
And it were glorious odds
For maiden slain, among
The equals of the Gods
In life—and then in death—to gain a place.

II. 1.

ANTIGONE.   They mock me. Gods of Thebes ! why scorn you me
Thus, to my face,
Alive, not death-stricken yet ?
O city, and you the city's large-dowered race,
Ye streams from Dirca's source,
Ye woods that shadow Theba's chariot-course,

---

[1] Niobe, from Phrygia in Asia Minor. Her children were killed by Apollo and Artemis after she had boasted of being a more prolific mother than theirs. In her sorrow she turned to stone on the mountain.

Listen and see,
    Let none of you forget,
How sacrificed, and for what laws offended,
By no tears friended,
    I to the prisoning mound
Of a strange grave am journeying under ground.
Ah me unhappy ! home is none for me ;
Alike in life or death an exile must I be.

CHORUS.   Thou to the farthest verge forth-faring,
    O my child, of daring,
    Against the lofty threshold of the laws
    Didst stumble and fall. The cause
    Is some ancestral load, which thou art bearing.

II. 2.

ANTIGONE.   There didst thou touch upon my bitterest bale—
    A threefold tale—
      My father's piteous doom,
    Doom of us all, scions of Labdacus.
      Woe for my mother's bed !
    Woe for the ill-starred spouse, from her own womb
    Untimely born !
      O what a father's house
    Was that from whence I drew my life forlorn !
    To whom, unwed,
      Accursed, lo I come
    To sojourn as a stranger in their home !
    And thou too, ruined, my brother, in a wife,
Didst by thy death bring death upon thy sister's life !

CHORUS.   To pay due reverence is a duty, too :
    And power—his power, whose empire is confest,
    May no wise be transgressed ;
    But thee thine own infatuate mood o'er-threw.

ANTIGONE.   Friendless, unwept, unwed,
                   I, sick at heart, am led
                     The way prepared for me ;
                       Day's hallowed orb on high
                   I may no longer see ;
                   For me no tears are spent,
                   Nor any friends lament
                       The death I die.

Enter CREON.

CREON.   Think you that any one, if help might be
In wailing and lament before he died,
Would ever make an end ? Away with her !
Wall her up close in some deep catacomb,
As I have said ; leave her alone, apart,
To perish, if she will ; or if she live,
To make her tomb her tenement. For us,
We will be guiltless of this maiden's blood ;
But here on earth she shall abide no more.
ANTIGONE.   Thou Grave, my bridal chamber ! dwelling-place
Hollowed in earth, the everlasting prison
Whither I bend my steps, to join the band
Of kindred, whose more numerous host already
Persephone hath counted with the dead ;
Of whom I last and far most miserably
Descend, before my term of life is full ;
I come, cherishing this hope especially,
To win approval in my father's sight,
Approval too, my mother, in thine, and thine
Dear brother ! for that with these hands I paid
Unto you dead lavement and ordering
And sepulchre-libations ; and that now,
Polynices, in the tendance of thy body
I meet with this reward. Yet to the wise
It was no crime, that I did honour thee.

For never had I, even had I been
Mother of children, or if spouse of mine
Lay dead and mouldering, in the state's despite
Taken this task upon me. Do you ask
What argument I follow here of law ?
One husband dead, another might be mine ;
Sons by another, did I lose the first ;
But, sire and mother buried in the grave,
A brother is a branch that grows no more.
Yet I, preferring by this argument
To honour thee to the end, in Creon's sight
Appear in that I did so to offend,
And dare to do things heinous, O my brother !
And for this cause he hath bid lay hands on me,
And leads me, not as wives or brides are led,
Unblest with any marriage, any care
Of children ; destitute of friends, forlorn,
Yet living, to the chambers of the dead
See me descend. Yet what celestial right
Did I transgress ?   How should I any more
Look up to heaven, in my adversity ?
Whom should I call to aid ?   Am I not come
Through piety to be held impious ?   If
This is approved in Heaven, why let me suffer,
And own that I have sinned ;   but if the sin
Belong to these—O may their punishment
Be measured by the wrongfulness of mine !

1 SENATOR.   Still the same storms possess her, with the same
          Precipitance of spirit.

CREON.   Then for this
          Her guards shall rue their slowness.

ANTIGONE.   Woe for me !
          The word I hear comes hand in hand with death !

1 SENATOR.   I may not say Be comforted, for this
   Shall not be so ;   I have no words of cheer.
ANTIGONE.   O City of Theba !   O my country !   Gods,
   The Fathers of my race !   I am led hence—
   I linger now no more. Behold me, lords,
   The last of your kings' house—what doom is mine,
   And at whose hands, and for what cause—that I
   Duly performed the dues of piety !

            [*Exeunt* ANTIGONE *and guards.*

CHORUS.

I. 1.

For a dungeon brazen-barred
 The body of Danae endured
  To exchange Heaven's daylight of old,
 In a tomb-like chamber immured,
Hid beneath fetter and guard ;
And she was born, we are told,
 O child, my child, unto honour,
 And a son[1] was begotten upon her
To Zeus in a shower of gold.
But the stress of a Fate is hard ;
Nor wealth, nor warfare, nor ward,
 Nor black ships cleaving the sea
 Can resist her, or flee.

I. 2.

And the Thracians' king, Dryas' son,[2]
 The hasty of wrath, was bound

---

[1] The hero Perseus.
[2] Lycurgus. In his madness he killed his wife and children.

For his words of mocking and pride ;
　Dionysus closing him round,
Pent in a prison of stone ;
Till, his madness casting aside
　Its flower and fury wild,
　He knew what God he reviled—
Whose power he had defied ;
Restraining the Mænad choir,[1]
Quenching the Evian[2] fire,
　Enraging the Muses' throng,
　The lovers of song.

II. 1.

And by the twofold main
　Of rocks Cyanean[3]—there
　　Lies the Bosporean strand,
And the lone Thracian plain
　Of Salmydessus, where
　　Is Ares' border-land :
Who saw the stab of pain
　Dealt on the Phineid pair[4]
　　At that fierce dame's command ;
Blinding the orbits of their blasted sight,
Smitten, without spear to smite,
　By a spindle's point made bare,
　And by a bloody hand.

---

[1] Wild female devotees of Dionysus.
[2] Dionysus'.
[3] The clashing rocks at the entrance to the Black Sea; all the geographical terms here indicate this area.
[4] The sons of Phineus, a local seer, who blinded them at the urging of his second wife, their stepmother. Their mother was Kleopatra, a daughter of Boreas, the north wind, and of an Athenian woman (a daughter of King Erectheus) whom he had abducted.

II. 2.

They mourned their mother dead,
   Their hearts with anguish wrung,
     Wasting away, poor seed
Of her deserted bed ;
   Who, Boreas' daughter, sprung
     From the old Erechtheid breed,
In remote caverns fed
   Her native gales among,
     Went swiftly as the steed,
Offspring of Heaven, over the steep-down wild ;
Yet to her too, my child,
   The Destinies, that lead
     Lives of long ages, clung.

Enter TIRESIAS *led by a boy.*

TIRESIAS.   Princes of Thebes, two fellow-travellers.
    Debtors in common to the eyes of one,
    We stand before you ; for a blind man's path
    Hangs on the guide who marshals him the way.
CREON.   What would'st thou now, reverend Tiresias ?
TIRESIAS.   That will I tell. Do thou obey the seer.
CREON.   I never have departed hitherto
    From thy advice.
TIRESIAS.   And therefore 'tis, thou steerest
    The city's course straight forward.
CREON.   Thou hast done me
    Good service, I can witness.
TIRESIAS.   Now again
    Think, thou dost walk on fortune's razor-edge.
CREON.   What is it ? I tremble but to see thee speak.
TIRESIAS.   Listen to what my art foreshadoweth,
    And thou shalt know. I lately, taking seat

On my accustomed bench of augury,
Whither all tribes of fowl after their kind
Alway resort, heard a strange noise of birds
Screaming with harsh and dissonant impetus ;
And was aware how each the other tore
With murderous talons ; for the whirr of wings
Rose manifest. Then feared I, and straight made trial
Of sacrifices on the altar-hearths
All blazing ; but, out of the offerings,
There sprang no flame ; only upon embers charred
Thick droppings melted off the thigh-pieces,
And heaved and sputtered, and the gall-bladders
Burst, and were lost, while from the folds of fat
The loosened thigh-bones fell. Such auguries,
Failing of presage through the unseemliness
Of holy rites, I gather from this lad,
Who is to me, as I to others, guide.
And this state-sickness comes by thy self-will ;
For all our hearths and altars are defiled
With prey of dogs and fowl, who have devoured
The dead unhappy son of Œdipus.
Therefore the Gods accept not of us now
Solemn peace-offering or burnt sacrifice,
Nor bird trills out a happy-boding note,
Gorged with the fatness of a slain man's blood.
This, then, my son, consider ; that to err
From the right path is common to mankind ;
But having erred, that mortal is no more
Losel or fool, who medicines the ill
Wherein he fell, and stands not obstinate.
Conceit of will savours of emptiness.
Give place, then, in the presence of the dead.
Wound not the life that's perished. Where's thy valour
In slaying o'er the slain ? Well I advise,

Meaning thee well ; 'tis pleasantest to learn
Of good advisers, when their words bring gain.
CREON.   Old man, ye all, like archers at a mark,
Are loosing shafts at me ; I am not spared
Even your soothsayers' practice ; by whose tribe
Long since have I been made as merchandize,
And bought, and sold.   Gather your gains at will !
Market your Sardian silver, Indian gold !
That man ye shall not cover with a tomb ;
Not though the eagle ministers of Jove
To Jove's own throne should bear their prey of him,
Not even for horror at such sacrilege
Will I permit his burial.   This I know ;
There is no power in any man to touch
The Gods with sacrilege ; but foul the falls
Which men right cunning fall, Tiresias—
Old man, I say—when for the sake of gain
They speak foul treason with a fair outside.
TIRESIAS.   Alas, does no man know, does no man think—
CREON.   What should one think ? What common saw is this ?
TIRESIAS.   How far good counsel passes all things good ?
CREON.   So far, I think, folly's the worst of harm !
TIRESIAS.   That is the infirmity that fills thy nature.
CREON.   I care not to retort upon thee, seer.
TIRESIAS.   Thou dost, thou say'st my oracles are false.
CREON.   All the prophetic tribe are covetous.
TIRESIAS.   And that of kings fond of disgraceful gain.
CREON.   Know'st thou of whom thou speak'st ?   I am thy lord.
TIRESIAS.   Yea, thou hast saved the state ; I gave it thee.
CREON.   Thou art a wise seer, but in love with wrong.
TIRESIAS.   Thou wilt impel me to give utterance
To my still dormant prescience.
CREON.   Say on ;
Only beware thou do not speak for gain.

TIRESIAS.   For gain of thine, methinks, I do not speak.

CREON.   Thou shalt not trade upon my wits, be sure.

TIRESIAS.   And be thou sure of this; thou shalt not tell
Many more turns of the sun's chariot-wheel,
Ere thou shalt render satisfaction, one
From thy own loins in payment, dead for dead,
For that thou hast made Life join hands with Death,
And sent a living soul unworthily
To dwell within a tomb, and keep'st a corpse
Here, from the presence of the Powers beneath,
Not for thy rights or any God's above,
But lawlessly in their despite usurped,
Unhallowed, disappointed, uninterred ;
Wherefore the late-avenging punishers,
Furies, from Death and Heaven, lay wait for thee,
To take thee in the evil of thine own hands.
Look to it, whether I be bribed who speak ;
For as to that, with no great wear of time,
Men's, women's wails to thine own house shall answer.
Also all cities rise in enmity,
To the strown relics of whose citizens
None pays due hallowing, save beasts of prey,
Dogs, or some fowl, whose pinions to their gates—
Yea, to each hearth—bear taint defiling them.
Such bolts, in wrath, since thou dar'st anger me,
I loosen at thy bosom, archer-like,
Sure-aimed, whose burning smart thou shalt not shun.
Lead me away, boy, to my own home again ;
And let him vent his spleen on younger men,
And learn to keep a tongue more gentle, and
A brain more sober, than he carries now.

[*Exeunt* TIRESIAS *and Boy.*

1 SENATOR.   The seer is gone, my lord, denouncing woe ;
      And from the day my old hairs began to indue
      Their white for black, we have known him for a watch
      Who never barked to warn the state in vain.
CREON.   I know it too ; and I am ill at ease ;
      'Tis bitter to submit ; but Até's[1] hand
      Smites bitterly on the spirit that abides her.
1 SENATOR.   Creon Menœceus' son, be wise at need !
CREON.   What should I do ?   speak, I will hearken.
1 SENATOR.   Go,
      Set free the maiden from the vault, and build
      A tomb for that dead outcast.
CREON.   You approve it ?
      You deem that I should yield ?
1 SENATOR.   Sir, with all speed.
      Swift-footed come calamities from Heaven
      To cut off the perverse.
CREON.   O God, 'tis hard !
      But I quit heart, and yield ; I cannot fight
      At odds with destiny.
1 SENATOR.   Up then, to work !
      Commit it not to others !
CREON.   I am gone
      Upon the instant.   Quickly, quickly, men,
      You and your fellows, get you, axe in hand,
      Up to the place, there, yonder ; and because
      I am thus minded, other than before,
      I who did bind her will be there to loose ;
      For it misgives me it is best to keep
      The old appointed laws, all our life long.
               [*Exeunt* CREON *and Attendants.*

---

[1] Goddess of retribution.

CHORUS.

I. 1.

Thou by many names addrest,
Child of Zeus loud-thundering,
Glory of a Theban maid, [1]
Who unbidden wanderest
   Fair Italia's King, [2]
And art lord in each deep glade
Whither all men seek to her,
Eleusinian Demeter ; [3]
Bacchus, who by soft-flowing waters
Of Ismenus[4] habitest
Theba, mother of Bacchant daughters,
With the savage Dragon's stock,

I. 2.

Thee the lurid wild-fire meets
O'er the double-crested rock,
Where Corycian[5] Nymphs arow
Bacchic-wise ascending go,
   Thee Castalia's[6] rill ;
Thee the ivy-covered capes
Usher forth of Nysa's hill, [7]

---

[1] Bacchus (Dionysus) was the son of Zeus and the Theban Semele, who died of the lightning flashes emanating from her divine lover.
[2] Because of the many grapevines there (?).
[3] Goddess of grain with a sanctuary at Eleusis, outside Athens.
[4] Local river.
[5] Named for a cave on Mount Parnassus, near Delphi.
[6] A spring on Parnassus.
[7] In Phocis, where Dionysus grew up.

And the shore with green of grapes
Clustering, where the hymn to thee
Rises up immortally,
Visitant in Theban Streets,
" Evoe, O Evoe ! "[1]

II. 1.

Wherefore, seeing thy City thus—
City far above all other
Dear to thee, and her, thy mother
Lightning-slain—by sickness grievous
Holden fast in all her gates,
Come with quickness to relieve us,
By the slopes of Parnasus,
    Or the roaring straits.

II. 2.

Hail to thee, the first advancing
In the stars' fire-breathing chorus !
Leader of the nightly strain,
Boy and son of Zeus and King !
Manifest thyself before us
With thy frenzied Thyiad[2] train,
Who their lord Iacchus[3] dancing
    Praise, and all night sing.

Enter a MESSENGER.

[1] Bacchic chant.
[2] Female devotees.
[3] Bacchus.

MESSENGER.   You citizens who dwell beside the roof
      Of Cadmus and Amphion,[1] there is no sort
      Of human life that I could ever praise,
      Or could dispraise, as constant ; Fortune still
      Raising and Fortune overthrowing still
      The happy and the unhappy ; and none can read
      What is set down for mortals.   Creon, methought
      Was enviable erewhile, when he preserved
      This land of Cadmus from its enemies,
      And took the country's absolute monarchy,
      And ruled it, flourishing with a noble growth
      From his own seed ; and now, he has lost all.
      For when men forfeit all their joys in life,
      One in that case I do not count alive,
      But deem of him as of some animate corse.
      Pile now great riches, if thou wilt, at home ;
      Wear thou the living semblance of a king ;
      An if delight be lacking, all the rest
      I would not purchase, as compared with joy,
      From any, for the shadow of a shade.
1 SENATOR.   What new affliction to the royal stock
      Com'st thou to tell ?
MESSENGER.   Death is upon them—death
      Caused by the living.
1 SENATOR.   And who is the slayer ?
      Speak ! who the victim ?
MESSENGER.   Hæmon is no more ;
      His life-blood spilt, and by no stranger's hand.
1 SENATOR.   What, by his father's, or his own ?
MESSENGER.   Self-slaughtered ;
      Wroth with his father for the maiden slain.
1 SENATOR.   Prophet ! how strictly is thy word come true!

---

[1] Amphion, husband of Niobe, and a builder of Thebes.

MESSENGER.   Look to the future, for these things are so.
1 SENATOR.   And I behold the poor Eurydice
          Come to us from the palace, Creon's wife ;
          Either of chance, or hearing her son's name.

Enter EURYDICE.

EURYDICE.   O all you citizens, I heard the sound
          Of your discourse, as I approached the gates,
          Meaning to bring my prayers before the face
          Of Pallas ; even as I undid the bolts,
          And set the door ajar, a voice of woe
          To my own household pierces through my ears ;
          And I sink backward on my handmaidens
          Afaint for terror ; but whate'er the tale,
          Tell it again ; I am no novice, I,
          In misery, that hearken.
MESSENGER.   Dear my mistress,
          I saw, and I will speak, and will let slip
          No syllable of the truth.   Why should we soothe
          Your ears with stories, only to appear
          Liars thereafter ?   Truth is alway right.
          —I followed in attendance on your lord,
          To the flat hill-top, where despitefully
          Was lying yet, harried by dogs, the body
          Of Polynices.   Pluto's name, and hers,
          The wayside goddess,[1] we invoked, to stay
          Their anger and be favourable ; and him
          We washed with pure lustration, and consumed
          On fresh-lopped branches the remains of him,
          And piled a monument of natal earth
          High over all ; thence to the maiden's cell,
          Chamber of death, with bridal couch of stone,

---

[1] Hecate, an underworld goddess.

We made as if to enter.   But afar
One fellow hears a loud uplifted wail
Fill all the unhallowed precinct ; comes, and tells
His master, Creon ; the uncertain sound
Of piteous crying, as he draws more nigh,
Comes round him, and he utters, groaning loud,
A lamentable plaint ; " Me miserable !
Was I a prophet ?   Is this path I tread
The unhappiest of all ways I ever went ?
My son's voice thrills my ear.   What ho, my guard !
Run quickly thither to the tomb where stones
Have been dragged down to make an opening,
Go in and look, whether I really hear
The voice of Hæmon, or am duped by Heaven. "
Quickly, at our distracted lord's command,
We looked : and in the tomb's inmost recess
Found we her, as she had been hanged by the neck,
Fast in a strip-like loop of linen ; and him
Laid by her, clasping her about the waist,
Mourning his wedlock severed in the grave,
And his sire's deeds, and his ill-fated bride.
He, when he sees them, with a terrible cry
Goes in towards him, calling out aloud
" Ah miserable, what hast thou done ?   what mind
Hadst thou ?   by what misfortune art thou crazed ?
Come out, my son,—suppliant I ask of thee ! "
But with fierce aspect the youth glared at him ;
Spat in his face ; answered him not a word ;
Grasped at the crossed hilts of his sword and drew it,
And—for the father started forth in flight—
Missed him ! then, angered with himself, poor fool,
There as he stood he flung himself along
Upon the sword-point firmly planted in
The middle of his breast, and, conscious yet,

Clings to the maid, clasped in his failing arms,
And gasping, sends forth on the pallid cheek
Fast welling drops of blood : So lies he, dead,
With his arms round the dead ; there, in the grave
His bridal rite is full ; his misery
Is witness to mankind what worst of woe
The lack of counsel brings a man to know !

                                     [*Exit* EURYDICE.

1 SENATOR.   What do you make of this ? The woman's gone
Back, and without one word, of good or bad !
MESSENGER.   I marvel too ; and yet I am in hope
She would not choose, hearing her son's sad fate,
In public to begin her keening-cry ;
But rather to her handmaids in the house
Dictate the mourning for a private pain.
She is not ignorant of self-control,
That she should err.
1 SENATOR.   I know not ; but on me
Weigh heavily both silence over-much,
And loud complaint in vain.
MESSENGER.   Well, we shall know it,
If she hide aught within a troubled heart
Even to suppression of its utterance,
If we approach the house. Yes, you say truly,
It does weigh heavy, silence over-much.

                                       [*Exit.*

CHORUS.

Lo now, Creon himself draws near us,
Clasping a record
Manifest, if we sin not, saying it,
Of ruin unwrought by the hands of others,
   But fore-caused by his own self-will.

Enter CREON, *attended, with the body of* HÆMON.

I. 1.

CREON.   O sins of a mind
                          That is minded to stray !
                     Mighty to bind
                          And almighty to slay !
          Behold us, kin slayers and slain, O ye who stand by the
             way !

                          Ah, newness of death !
                             O my fruitless design !
                        New to life's breath,
                             O son that wert mine,
          Ah, ah, thou art dead, thou art sped, for a fault that was
             mine, not thine !

1 SENATOR.   Ah, how thou seem'st to see the truth, too late !
CREON.   Ah yes, I have learnt, I know my wretchedness !

II. 1.

                     Heaviness hath o'ertaken me
                          And mine head the rod ;
                     The roughness hath shaken me
                          Of the paths I trod ;
          Woe is me !   my delight is brought low, cast under the feet
             of a God !

                Woe for man's labours that are profitless !

Re-enter the MESSENGER.

MESSENGER.   O master, now thou hast and hast in store
                     Of sorrows ; one thou bearest in thine arms,

And one at home thou seemest to be come
Merely to witness.

CREON.   And what more of sorrow,
Or what more sorrowful, is yet behind ?

MESSENGER.   Thy wife, the mother—mother of the dead—
Is, by a blow just fallen, haplessly slain.

I. 2.

CREON.   O hard to appease thee,
                    Haven of Death,
                How should it please thee
                    To end this breath ?
O herald of heavy news, what is this thy mouth uttereth ?

                O man, why slayest thou
                    A man that is slain ?
                Alas, how sayest thou
                    Anew and again
That the slaying of a woman is added to slaying—a pain to
    a pain ?

MESSENGER.   See for thyself ; the palace doors unclose.

The Altar is disclosed, with the dead body of EURYDICE.

CREON.   Woe is me again, for this new sorrow I see.

II. 2.

                What deed is not done ?
                    What tale is not told ?
                Thy body, O son,
                    These arms enfold—

> Dead—wretch that I am !   Dead, too, is the face these eyes
>   behold.
>
> Ah, child, for thy poor mother !   ah for thee !

MESSENGER.   She with a sharp-edged dagger in her heart
            Lies at the altar ; and her darkened lids
            Close on her wailing for the glorious lot
            Of Megareus,[1] who died before, and next
            For his, and last, upon her summoning
            Evil to fall on thee, the child-slayer !

III. 1.

CREON.   Alas, I faint for dread !
                    Is there none will deal
                A thrust that shall lay me dead
                    With the two-edged steel ?
                Ah woe is me !
                I am all whelmed in utter misery !

MESSENGER.   It may be so ; thou art arraigned of her
            Who here lies dead, for the occasion thou
            Hast wrought for Destiny on her, and him.
1 SENATOR.   In what way did she slay herself and die ?
MESSENGER.   Soon as she heard the raising of the wail
            For her son's death, she stabbed herself to the heart.

IV. 1.

CREON.   Woe is me !   to none else can they lay it,
             This guilt, but to me !

---

[1] Her husband before Creon (?).

I, I was the slayer, I say it,
    Unhappy, of thee !
O bear me, haste ye, spare not,
    To the ends of earth,
More nothing than they who were not
    In the hour of birth !

1 SENATOR.   Thou counsellest well—if anything be well
    To follow, in calamity ; the ills
    Lying in our path, soonest o'erpast, were best.

III. 2.

CREON.   Come, thou most welcome Fate,
           Appear, O come ;
         Bring my days' final date,
           Fill up their sum !
         Come quick, I pray ;
         Let me not look upon another day !

1 SENATOR.   This for to-morrow ; we must take some thought
    On that which lies before us ; for these griefs,
    They are their care on whom the care has fallen.
CREON.   I did but join your prayer for our desire.
1 SENATOR.   Pray thou for nothing more ; there is no respite
    To mortals from the ills of destiny.

IV. 2.

CREON.   Lead me forth, cast me out, no other
           Than a man undone ;
         Who did slay, unwitting, thy mother
           And thee, my son !

I turn me I know not where
    For my plans ill-sped,
And a doom that is heavy to bear
    Is come down on my head.

        [*Exit* CREON, *attended.*

CHORUS.

Wisdom first for a man's well-being
Maketh, of all things.   Heaven's insistence
Nothing allows of man's irreverence ;
And great blows great speeches avenging,
    Dealt on a boaster,
Teach men wisdom in age, at last.

        [*Exeunt omnes.*

DOVER·THRIFT·EDITIONS

PLAYS

THE MIKADO, William Schwenck Gilbert. 64pp. 27268-0
FAUST, PART ONE, Johann Wolfgang von Goethe. 192pp. 28046-2
THE INSPECTOR GENERAL, Nikolai Gogol. 80pp. 28500-6
SHE STOOPS TO CONQUER, Oliver Goldsmith. 80pp. 26867-5
A DOLL'S HOUSE, Henrik Ibsen. 80pp. 27062-9
GHOSTS, Henrik Ibsen. 64pp. 29852-3
HEDDA GABLER, Henrik Ibsen. 80pp. 26469-6
THE WILD DUCK, Henrik Ibsen. 96pp. 41116-8
VOLPONE, Ben Jonson. 112pp. 28049-7
DR. FAUSTUS, Christopher Marlowe. 64pp. 28208-2
THE MISANTHROPE, Molière. 64pp. 27065-3
ANNA CHRISTIE, Eugene O'Neill. 80pp. 29985-6
BEYOND THE HORIZON, Eugene O'Neill. 96pp. 29085-9
THE EMPEROR JONES, Eugene O'Neill. 64pp. 29268-1
THE LONG VOYAGE HOME AND OTHER PLAYS, Eugene O'Neill. 80pp. 28755-6
RIGHT YOU ARE, IF YOU THINK YOU ARE, Luigi Pirandello. 64pp. (Not available in Europe
   or United Kingdom.) 29576-1
SIX CHARACTERS IN SEARCH OF AN AUTHOR, Luigi Pirandello. 64pp. (Not available in
   Europe or United Kingdom.) 29992-9
PHÈDRE, Jean Racine. 64pp. 41927-4
HANDS AROUND, Arthur Schnitzler. 64pp. 28724-6
ANTONY AND CLEOPATRA, William Shakespeare. 128pp. 40062-X
AS YOU LIKE IT, William Shakespeare. 80pp. 40432-3
HAMLET, William Shakespeare. 128pp. 27278-8
HENRY IV, William Shakespeare. 96pp. 29584-2
JULIUS CAESAR, William Shakespeare. 80pp. 26876-4
KING LEAR, William Shakespeare. 112pp. 28058-6
LOVE'S LABOUR'S LOST, William Shakespeare. 64pp. 41929-0
MACBETH, William Shakespeare. 96pp. 27802-6
MEASURE FOR MEASURE, William Shakespeare. 96pp. 40889-2
THE MERCHANT OF VENICE, William Shakespeare. 96pp. 28492-1
A MIDSUMMER NIGHT'S DREAM, William Shakespeare. 80pp. 27067-X
MUCH ADO ABOUT NOTHING, William Shakespeare. 80pp. 28272-4
OTHELLO, William Shakespeare. 112pp. 29097-2
RICHARD III, William Shakespeare. 112pp. 28747-5
ROMEO AND JULIET, William Shakespeare. 96pp. 27557-4
THE TAMING OF THE SHREW, William Shakespeare. 96pp. 29765-9
THE TEMPEST, William Shakespeare. 96pp. 40658-X
TWELFTH NIGHT; OR, WHAT YOU WILL, William Shakespeare. 80pp. 29290-8
ARMS AND THE MAN, George Bernard Shaw. 80pp. (Not available in Europe or United
   Kingdom.) 26476-9
HEARTBREAK HOUSE, George Bernard Shaw. 128pp. (Not available in Europe or United
   Kingdom.) 29291-6
PYGMALION, George Bernard Shaw. 96pp. (Available in U.S. only.) 28222-8
THE RIVALS, Richard Brinsley Sheridan. 96pp. 40433-1
THE SCHOOL FOR SCANDAL, Richard Brinsley Sheridan. 96pp. 26687-7
ANTIGONE, Sophocles. 64pp. 27804-2
OEDIPUS AT COLONUS, Sophocles. 64pp. 40659-8
OEDIPUS REX, Sophocles. 64pp. 26877-2